k. l. mahon

just one tear

Lothrop, Lee & Shepard Books   New York

just one tear

march 2

I walked through the long corridors of the hospital with my mother today. Floor 3. Ward 16. Bed 2. My father is there. The father who used to play soccer and baseball with me. Now he's doing something more important. Dying.

My mother bustled me into his room. Not a word came from those very gossipy lips of hers. Not much has come from those lips for days now.

A quick smile came to my face when I first saw my father, but it soon left as I realized I couldn't rush over to him and tell him about my day at school. All I could do was watch. Watch his glazed eyes stare into the distance. The distance that isn't there.

I didn't know what I was doing there. He didn't know I was there. I wanted to say something to him, and I wanted him to respond.

Mom told me it would be good for me and that I shouldn't be scared to cry. Shouldn't be embarrassed. But I couldn't cry. I know that if I did, it wouldn't be for Dad. It would be for myself. He isn't suffering. He isn't hurting or feeling. He's just lying there in his own world. His own silent, uninterrupted world of nothing. He's very peaceful. I'm the one suffering. My family and I. But it's not right when we don't put him first.

march 3

It's my birthday today. No party. No presents. Just a weak kiss and a soft "Happy Birthday" from my mother.

I visited my father today — not a very nice thing to do on your birthday.

Nothing has changed. Still those glazed eyes and those tubes. Those tubes I can't bear to look at. Especially when they're sticking into my father's 41-year-old body. My father — who coached our school soccer team, who made all my friends envy me.

I didn't go to school again today. I'm not looking forward to going. I don't think I can bear everyone looking at me and feeling sorry for me.

march 4

My mother cried today. Those tears rolling down her cheeks told me what I'd feared for the past week. Tears of fear. Tears of death.

I didn't know what to do. I didn't know what to say. No tears fell from my eyes. I didn't even feel upset.

I put an awkward arm around my mother. No sound came from my lips. There were many things I wanted to say. They were sitting in my mind, pushing to get out, but I didn't say them. Any of them. It was much easier not to bother. To keep quiet.

"I'm sorry," my mother said softly, knowing I knew what she had to tell me.

We sat on the edge of the bed. My mother crying softly. No sobs. No long, heaving sighs. Just a soft, quiet whimpering. Me, no tears, just silence. I looked at the two of us in the mirror. My mother's reflection was highlighted by her red, puffy eyes. My reflection looked normal.

No sad eyes. No sad face.

The person I loved most in the world was gone, and I looked normal. I wanted to be sad. To satisfy myself. To destroy the guilt. But I couldn't.

march 5

I went to school today. Not everybody knew about my father. One of the boys on the soccer team asked me where he was. I said nothing.

I didn't speak much today. Just the odd word. I didn't raise my hand to answer any questions. I didn't talk with my friends. I didn't even play soccer. It was a very silent day for me.

march 7

I didn't write yesterday. We went to our regular restaurant. It felt funny, just the two of us. No Dad to joke around with.

The funeral was today. "Always remembered. Always with God. Always at peace."

I looked at my feet during the whole service. I said nothing. I heard nothing. I did nothing. I blocked myself from the rest of the world. All I did was remember. Remember the time when he picked me up and kissed me after I scored on my first try. Remember all the good times when he was there. Always there. Now he was stuck in the ground in a wooden box. He would never be there for me again.

march 8

I went to the beach today. I just sat and looked at the waves.

Maybe the waves are like what my father was doing when he was dying. Coming in, going out. Coming in, going out. Maybe one day they'll all be gone. Just like my father.

I'm sitting now, in my bedroom, wishing I was still at the beach. There I had the company of sea gulls and sandpipers. Here I have no company. My mother is no company. She's hollow. Just a shell. No thoughts. No feelings.

Here I can hear the hall clock ticking, hear its endless droning sound. It's like my mother. Always the same speed. Not like my father. He's always different. Sometimes fast, sometimes slow. My father is still ticking. I wonder if it'll ever stop, his ticking. He's still in me. I think now his ticking is fast. Memories of him keep running around my head. Faster than they ever did before.

march 9

We found out the trial date today. March 20. I'm the only eyewitness.

I went to the beach again today. I just sat for most of the time. The sand was warm and comforting. The seagulls talked to me in their special way.

I stood on the rocks, watching the waves break at my feet.

I stood, hoping a wave would pick me up and take me away so I could be lost forever. But it didn't.

march 11

Today is Saturday. Dad's day. We packed all of his belongings into a box. Mom cried a little.

I didn't comfort her. I didn't hug her. I didn't talk to her. I just sat and watched her cry.

I went to the movies yesterday. Mom said it would be good to get out some more with my friends. We went to a comedy. My friends said it was very funny. Was it? I can't remember what it was about.

march 12

I didn't go to the beach today. Instead I went to the grave. "Always remembered. Always with God. Always at peace." I sat on Dad's grave. I suppose it may have seemed ungrateful and disrespectful, but I sat on it anyway.

I sat and thought. Tried to work out my anger, my guilt, my sadness.

I'm angry at myself. I could've saved my father. I'm angry at *him,* whoever he is — the man who killed my father. I'd like to kill him.

I'm also sad. Not sad like my mother. She's sad on the outside. I'm sad on the inside. Fighting inside. Fighting my fear of the trial. Fighting my anger. Fighting my sadness. Fighting my guilt. They're all coming at me together, all at once. Like a pack of angry dogs.

march 14

I went to the beach again. Today it wasn't quiet like before. There was someone else there. He came over quickly but quietly and sat next to me.

He was the first to say something. "Hi!" he said cheerfully. It made me sick. How could anyone be so happy?

I said "Hi!" and that was it for me. I said no more, but he talked on. He told me about himself. About his family. About his problems. Like me, he has real problems. I tried to work out whose were worse, his or mine. I'm still trying.

march 15

I saw my friend again today. He sat next to me. He didn't talk as much today, although he talked more than I did. Maybe he's almost talked himself out. I could tell he wanted me to talk. I told him my name. He asked me why I came to the beach so often. I didn't tell him. I promised myself I would never tell him. It's too hard. It's my secret. It's my problem. It's a problem even my mother doesn't know about. She could never understand. It's not my father's death. My problem is me. It's the way I handle this loss. *That* is my problem. It isn't normal. In my own eyes, I'm not normal. But I suppose I'll never change. That's just me.

march 19

I went to Dad's grave today. I've made it a Sunday ritual now.

I talked to him. He didn't talk to me, but I knew he was listening. I told him my fears. My fears about tomorrow. My fears about the next few days. My fears about court.

My mother has gone to see Dad a lot. I can tell by all the flowers piled up against the marker with his name on it. I don't take flowers. I don't take anything.

I haven't written for the last few days because my mother and I have spent most of our time at the lawyer's office going over the case. I don't talk much in there either. Only when I'm asked.

....

It was horrible today. The witness stand is horrible. The court is horrible. *He* is horrible.

I was second on the witness stand. The first was Dad's doctor, who examined him after he died. It was almost unbearable to hear him talk about my father like that. Like he was empty. Just an object. Not a human being.

Not someone who had feelings.

I remember my name being called. I remember sitting on the witness stand. My lawyer asked me questions first. Easy questions. Straightforward questions.

Then *his* lawyer came straight for me. Ready to attack. His words are still clear to me. Those sharp, painful words.

"How far away were you from your father's killer?" was his first question.

"I don't know."

"You don't know," he said, raising his voice. "I ask again. How far away from your father's killer were you?"

"About five yards," I answered quickly, taking a guess.

"Do you have any vision problems?"

"Objection!" my lawyer shouted, standing up.

"Objection overruled."

"Do you have any vision problems?" he asked again.

"Yes," I answered.

"Were you wearing your glasses at the time of the murder?"

"No."

"How do you know it was this man, then?"

"I don't know."

"I ask again," he said, nearly yelling, "how do you know it was *this* man?"

Then I fainted.

Now I'm in the foyer. Here it's quiet. I'm alone at last. Alone with my anger. Anger at that man. That man who drove me crazy until I fainted.

The trial is still going on, but I don't want to go back in there. It's worse than hell in there.

. . . .

I didn't go to court today. My mother said I'd get into trouble with the judge, but she can't make me go.

I went to the beach instead. My friend was there.

I prayed for the first time in my life last night. I prayed for myself. I prayed for my father. I prayed for my mother.

Tears rolled down my mother's face again last night. I walked into her room and saw her holding Dad's photo, running her hand up and down his face. She was calling his name.

I'm starting to understand my mother's kind of sorrow. Her way to deal with loss.

She'll never understand my sorrow. She thinks I have none. She thinks I'm just a kid. Just a kid who knew his father for only thirteen years. She thinks thirteen years isn't a very long time to get to love someone. To love someone enough to be sad when he's lost. She's wrong.

march 22

I went to court today. The judge said nothing. Nothing to me, anyway.

I was called up to the witness stand again. By *his* lawyer. My legs shook as I walked toward the witness stand. They shouldn't have. I'd already planned my answers to every question I could think of.

It wasn't as bad in there today. I suppose it was about equal to hell this time. I won't be called to testify again. Tomorrow we'll find out the verdict.

march 23

I'm angry tonight — the kind of anger where I want to kill someone. Anyone.

My mother is angry, but her anger is different from mine. Her anger is mixed up with her sadness. It's a terrible kind of anger.

My father is probably angry, too, but his anger is calmer than ours.

We didn't eat supper tonight. We couldn't.

I'm angry at God. I have no faith in Him. I know that's wrong, to lose your faith in God. But I have. First He took away my father. Then He didn't listen to my prayers. I asked Him to do one simple thing. He didn't do it. He didn't answer my prayer.

I'm driven to this anger by two words. Two words that are pretty unimportant when they're by themselves. Together they're horrible. They make my brain run around in circles and my heart beat faster. They make me want to scream, and that's what I did. As soon as I heard those two words I stood up and screamed. My longest, loudest, harshest scream — to let all my anger out, to set it all free.

But it hasn't gone completely. It's sitting in my mind. Gradually building up. Trying to take me over. I'm trying to make it leave. It won't. It's found a home and doesn't want to leave it. It'll never leave.

....

I'm sick today. My mother is crying. She's been crying all day, all night. She isn't worried about me. She doesn't care.

If my father were here...no, I shouldn't think too much about my father. It's hard, trying not to think about him. He's part of me. He'll always be part of me.

But *he* is free. That man. It hasn't been permanent for him. For Dad, though, it *has* been permanent. Very permanent. It's also permanent for us. The loss is permanent. The memories are permanent. The sorrow is permanent.

....

I saw my friend today. He looked different. He looked sad. He didn't talk as much today. I think I talked more than he did. I asked him what was wrong. He said nothing. Just silence.

I think it would be good to live in a silent world. No voices. No cars. No people. Nothing. But my friend doesn't live in a silent world. He lives in a noisy world. Probably noisier than mine. His world is dark. Like my sorrow and loss, his darkness is permanent.

My friend's problem has been with him since birth. Mine hasn't. His problem isn't as bad as mine. Well, I don't think it is.

He can live with his problem. He *has* lived with his problem. He *is living* with his problem. I haven't even tried living with mine yet.

As I sat on the beach today, I wondered. Wondered about God. Why did He do terrible things like this to us? We hadn't done anything wrong. We didn't deserve this. Any of it.

march 28

I made a fool of myself today. At school. It was noisy there. Completely opposite to the silence I crave. I couldn't handle it, all the noise. I stood up and screamed. Then ran. Ran home to my silent bedroom. I couldn't stand all the happy voices. I'm not going back there again. I've promised myself.

march 29

I'm scared for my friend tonight. I'm sure I heard him say he was going to kill himself. At the beach last night. He said it quietly, but I'm sure I heard it.

I didn't go to the beach today. I spent my whole day in this room. I ate no food. Drank nothing. Hibernating.

march 30

I broke my promise today. I went to school. No one said anything to me. They said things about me, though. I could see them whispering. I didn't hear their voices, but I knew what they were saying.

My mother is getting better. She hasn't cried very often lately. I think she's handling it better than I am.

april 1

My friend is dead. It happened last night. He jumped off the cliff.

I'm wondering which is worse now. My father's death or my friend's. I think it's my father's. I knew him longer.

At least my friend *wanted* to leave his life. Away from his family. Away from his friends.

My father would have liked to keep his life, I think. *We* would have liked to keep his life. God took him without permission. Without *his* permission. Without *our* permission.

It's April Fools' Day today. It's supposed to be happy. Not for me.

april 2

I went to the beach today. I was alone.
Alone with myself. Alone with the wind and
the waves. Even the gulls have deserted me.
I missed my friend.

I studied the cliff. The cliff that helped take
my friend's life. I watched the waves break
below it. It would be hard, I think, to take
your life like that. To just jump.

april 3

I was sent to the school counselor today. I sat. He talked. Not a word came from my mouth. Not a single word.

He talked on and on, mostly about his family. It was good in there with him. Just his voice. No background noise. No screaming. No murmuring. Just his soft, soothing voice. I'll be going there often now, I think.

april 4

I'm there now. In the school counselor's office. He said I could do what I wanted, so I'm writing. He's asking me questions, but I'm not answering. His questions are too hard to answer. They're all mixed up. Or maybe it's me who's all mixed up. I don't know.

april 6

My mother is sending me to my Aunt Sue's
house. She needs time on her own, she says.
She's selfish. I'm angry. I'm wondering
which is stronger, my anger or my sadness.
Before, it was my sadness. Now, I don't
know. My anger is trying to take over.

I was thinking last night. About everything.
Life. *My* life. I think I'd like to do what my
friend did. Jump. I couldn't be selfish like
that, though. In one way it would be good
for me. I could see my father again. But it
wouldn't be good for my mother.

I dream about my father often now. Sometimes the dreams are good, sometimes
they're bad, sometimes they're nightmares.

When they're good, I'm meeting him in
heaven. These are my favorite dreams.

When they're bad, I dream of arguments, fights.

When they're nightmares, I dream of memories. A gun. A blast. A face. A puddle of blood. My father dying. And then I wake up screaming. I'm covered in sweat. Sometimes I'm yelling, "Dad, don't go!"

april

I'm at Aunt Sue's house now. My mother isn't here. She's at home. Alone. Dwelling on herself. Not caring about anyone else. Least of all me.

At the dinner table tonight, they told me I was taking this all very well. But they don't know, do they? Only *I* know.

They know my outer self. Only I know my inner self. They don't know my sorrow. My anger. My guilt. They don't know the conflict inside me. The arguments. The fights. The cruel, horrible fights.

april 10

My relatives took me to the beach today. They took me because they wanted me not to think about Dad. They wanted me to enjoy myself. It was fun.

It was the first time I've forgotten about my father since his death. The first time I've had fun. It may have been only for a few hours, but I'm very grateful. They're all so kind to me. They love me more than my mother does. I wish I could live here forever.

april 11

I went to school today. Aunt Sue is very worried about my education. I spent the whole day with the school counselor. He asked me to call him Bill. He said we can become better friends that way, but I don't want to become better friends. Not with him.

He asked me if he could read my diary. I said no. I felt like he was taking advantage of this friendship we're supposed to have. Even though he asked only once, I know he's very curious. But I'll never give it to him. Never.

My cousins and aunt are going away. On vacation out west. At first I thought it was bad that they were going because I'd have to go back to my mother. Now it's good — they've asked me to go with them. Aunt Sue will ask my mother. I hope I can go.

april 12

I don't understand my mother. I'll never understand her. I don't know how she understands herself. Maybe she doesn't.

I'm not going on vacation with my cousins. How *could* she? How could she pass me off to my aunt because "she can't handle it," and then, when I might possibly be able to enjoy myself with them, she says I can't go?

Maybe she's jealous. Jealous of what? Jealous of me. Why? I don't know. I'll always be wondering.

She's changing, my mother. Changing every day. She's been changing ever since *that* day. That day of death. When all this changing is over, she'll be very evil. Very jealous. I may not love her anymore.

april 13

I don't feel like writing today. I'm not speaking to my mother.

april 14

I went to my father's grave today. Should I still say "my father"? I suppose so.

It's been ages since I visited him. We talked for a long time today.

I told him about Mom. I wonder if he's upset with her. Maybe not. Maybe he's selfish too. Maybe he doesn't care that I have to put up with her, as long as he doesn't.

Maybe nobody cares.

I have no friends now. It's like that song, "Nobody likes me. Everybody hates me." That's true for me, I think. Although I don't think *everyone* hates me. They just don't *like* me. There is a difference.

It's funny, you know, how when horrible things like this happen to you, when you most need other people, they all turn against you. I mean, it's not as if I killed him.

Well, not directly.

It's fear, I think. The reason they've all turned against me. Fear of what to say. Fear of what *I* might say. Fear is a horrible thing. It creates many problems.

april 16

My mother has been crying a lot lately. She seems to be in some kind of cycle. I wonder if she'll get better soon. I hope so. I can't stand to hear her cry so much — feeling sorry for herself. As soon as I hear her start, I leave. Leave for the beach. Leave for the grave. Leave for the church.

It has been more than a month now since my father's death. It's funny how they cling, my feelings of anger, guilt, and sadness. They'll probably be clinging forever.

april 17

I got a postcard from Aunt Sue today.

Wish you were here.
Lots of love,
Aunt Sue and the kids

It feels good to be loved. Before, when Dad
was alive, I took love for granted. Now it's
special.

I suppose Mom loves me too. In her own
special way. I wish, I wish.

That card showed me how much I really
missed them. I would never miss my mother
that much. I would never miss the jealousy
and self-centeredness that's so strong in her.
Never.

april 20

....

Aunt Sue got back today. I asked Mom if I could go and stay with them. She didn't answer, but I'm going anyway. I'm packing my bags now. I can't wait to get there. Where all the happiness is.

I went to school today. He asked me again. The counselor. To look at my diary. I promised myself before, and I'm promising myself again: Never!

It's my mother's birthday soon. Should I get her a present? Strangers don't give each other presents. That's what we are. Strangers.

Best friends — that's what we were. Then we grew apart. Grew apart so much that we became strangers. Strangers from two different worlds. Sometimes I wish we were friends again. Other times I'm glad we aren't. It's hard to be friends with someone who's so selfish. Very hard.

april 22

I bought my mother a present today. A bracelet. I hope she appreciates it. I also bought a card. Just a To and a From. Not like it used to be. Before, it was To Dear...Lots of Love From...and heaps of hugs and kisses. It's not like that anymore.

Just a To and From sounds cold, doesn't it? Icy cold. Well, maybe that's what she deserves.

You're supposed to give people presents because you love them. I'm giving my mother a present because I feel I should. So many things aren't what they should be, aren't they?

Maybe I *do* love my mother. If I really looked hard, deep down, maybe I'd find that love. I've tried looking deep down before — to find out about myself. I haven't found that love yet.

april 23

I went to the beach today. All my friends were there — the gulls and the sandpipers. I think they were surprised to see me.

It's been a long time. I'd forgotten the way the waves hit the sand. Today they seemed angry.

When I got home (I call it my home now), Aunt Sue was angry. She said they'd been worried about me. I should've told them where I was going. She was right. I *am* insensitive.

They don't know where I go to try to get rid of my anger. Now that I think about it, nobody knows except my dead friend. And my gulls and sandpipers. My mother never knew. All those nights I came home late. Did she ever worry? No.

april 24

Today is my mother's birthday. We went to the house. I didn't speak to her. She didn't speak to me. She avoided me.

I gave her a kiss when I gave her the present. An obligatory kiss. Then she disappeared. I heard muffled sobbing coming from her bedroom, but I wasn't about to go in and comfort her. I'm no good at that. Am I?

Most of the evening I sat outside with my cousins. Feeling guilty. Knowing that she was in there. Being sad.

I wonder why she still cries. I thought she'd be all dry by now. He's gone. Can't she see that all her crying won't help? Won't help anyone.

april 25

I went to school today, but I didn't visit the counselor. It felt funny, spending a whole day in class. I can't remember what it was like before, when I had friends. I can't even imagine what it would be like to have friends now.

Aunt Sue is calling me. She says my mother is on the phone. I don't want to go, but do I have any choice?

My mother was tearful again. Before I got on, Aunt Sue told me to give her a chance. Listen to what she has to say. So I did. She wants me to come home. She said she's sorry.

"What for?" I asked. But I knew what for. Manners make you say some funny things. So I'm going home. To live with a stranger.

april 26

My mother hasn't shed a single tear today. I even saw something very rare — so rare I haven't seen it in weeks. A smile. A warm, welcoming smile. It wasn't fake — not like the smiles people give me at school. No, this smile was real. And contagious. I suppose all real smiles are contagious, especially when they're from someone you used to really love. It showed me that, maybe, I could try again.

I used to see those smiles a lot before. It's funny, isn't it? The way I talk about Before. It sounds like Before is a different world. Well, maybe it is. Everyone is different now. My friends. My relatives. Everyone. The only person who hasn't changed is my father.

. . . .

My mother didn't cry today. I told her it was a record. She laughed. It was an uneasy laugh. Fighting off nervousness. Is this an improvement? I suppose so.

She keeps saying she's sorry. Sorry for being so...so selfish. I couldn't have put it better myself. But manners made me say, "You haven't been selfish." Is that a sin? Lying? Lying for the sake of someone else's feelings? Tell me, someone. I need to know.

I have no one to answer these questions now. I think many people know the answers, but they won't tell me. It's frustrating.

Dad knows. He wants to tell me, but they won't let him. My sandpipers know, but they won't tell me. They're too wise. My gulls know, and they...well, they try.

I always seem to be leaving my mother out.

Except when I'm complaining about her. Reading back, I can see I've been hard on her. She hasn't been a wonderful mother over the past month, but she has a right to be sad, doesn't she?

april 28

I did something amazing tonight. Amazing for me, anyway. It was one of those things you don't know you're going to do until you've done it. I kissed my mother and told her I loved her. I wasn't just telling her, I was telling myself. Reassuring myself.

I saw a tear in her eye. I wonder if it was a happy tear. I hope so.

I went to the grave today. I tried to sort myself out. Tried to put all my feelings into separate boxes. Sort of like moving house. It didn't work very well.

I was thinking about what I wrote the other night. About how I think I've been hard on my mother. It's funny, isn't it? How your feelings can change so quickly, so deeply. It's all a mystery to me. I wish I could understand life. It would be much easier to live then, wouldn't it?

may 2

Bill gave me homework tonight: What is
death?
I wrote,

> Death is silence.
> Death is lonely.
> Death is loss.
> Death is sometimes selfish.

As my pen scratched my homework on the
page, I felt a cold tickling on my cheek. A
tear. A single, wet tear. It dropped silently
onto the paper.
I learned something from that tear. I
learned that sometimes you can be sure you
know everything about the way you feel,

then suddenly you can realize that you're wrong. Deep down, what you find is not what you expected. Everything is very different.

As I looked at that tear, I whispered, "That was for you, Dad."